This book belongs to
my friend:

_____

A NOTE TO PARENTS

Most children love animals. Children are natural mimics, so they enjoy imitating the unique noises and movements of all sorts of creatures. In *Animal Parade*, Dora meets a variety of intriguing animals. Invite your child to join them and Dora on their amusing journey! As each new animal is introduced in the story, encourage your child to copy its movement. Hop with the frog, slither with the snake, and paddle with the duck!

Animal Parade is a wonderful story to read aloud to a group. Assign each child one of the characters in the story, and as the story unfolds, watch the children form their own parade. There are also many opportunities to make funny noises. Encourage your child and her friends to be as loud, goofy, and creative as they can. Together, the movements and noises will make the reading experience a very active one.

After reading the story, have the children choose their favorite animal, and make animal masks or costumes. March around your home or yard or have the children write and dramatize a new animal story. You may want to complete your celebration with milk and animal crackers.

Learning Fundamental: 🏃 **physical**

For more parent and kid-friendly activities, go to www.nickjr.com.

Animal Parade

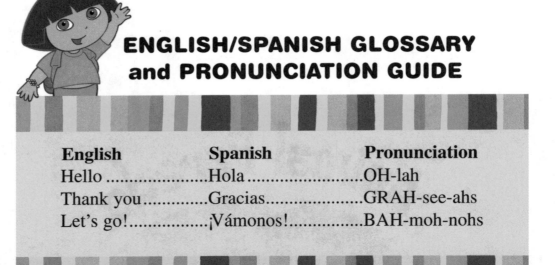

ENGLISH/SPANISH GLOSSARY and PRONUNCIATION GUIDE

English	Spanish	Pronunciation
Hello	Hola	OH-lah
Thank you	Gracias	GRAH-see-ahs
Let's go!	¡Vámonos!	BAH-moh-nohs

Published by Scholastic Inc., 90 Old Sherman Turnpike, Danbury, CT 06816

SCHOLASTIC and associated logos are trademarks and/or registered trademarks of Scholastic Inc.

ISBN 0-7172-6633-8

Printed in the U.S.A.

First Scholastic Printing, June 2003

Animal Parade

by
Christine Ricci

illustrated by
Tom Mangano

SCHOLASTIC INC.

New York Toronto London Auckland Sydney
Mexico City New Delhi Hong Kong Buenos Aires

One day, Dora was sitting on her front porch when Boots swung down from a nearby tree.

"Today is the Animal Parade!" he said excitedly. "There will be colorful floats, big balloons, and lots and lots of animals."

"Oh, I love the Animal Parade!" said Dora.

"Do you know the way to the Animal Parade?" Boots asked Dora.

"No," she said. "Let's ask Map. Map always helps us when we don't know which way to go."

"Map! Map!" called Dora and Boots.

Map peeked out of Backpack's side pocket.

"*Hola*, Map!" Dora said. "Can you help us get to the Animal Parade?"

"Sure," Map replied. "First you go through the Jungle, then you cross the Pond, and then you go over the Rocky Canyon. That's how to get to the Animal Parade."

"*Gracias,*" said Dora.

"I wonder which path leads to the Jungle," said Dora.

"I'll swing up to the top of the tree to see," said Boots. "*Swing! Swing! Swing!*"

"Great idea," Dora said. "Do you see the Jungle?"

Swing!

Swing! Swing!

March!
March!
March!

"The Jungle is that way!" Boots
called pointing to the green path.
He and Dora followed the green
path toward the Jungle. "We're going
to the Animal Parade!" they cheered.

"¡*Vámonos!* Let's go!" called Dora. "I'm going to march to the parade! *March! March! March!*"

"*Swing! Swing! Swing!*" called Boots from the trees.

When they reached the Jungle, Dora and Boots saw lots of mud!

"Oh, no!" cried Boots. "How will we get across the mud?"

Just then a little frog hopped out of a puddle and said, "You can hop like me! Just hop from rock to rock across the mud."

Dora said, "Great idea! Let's hop like a frog. *Hop! Hop! Hop!*"

After they hopped through the Jungle, Dora invited the frog to go with them to the Animal Parade. Everyone started down the road toward the Pond.

Swing! Swing! Swing!

Hop! Hop! Hop!

"We're going to the Animal Parade!" croaked the frog.

March!
March!
March!

"Oh, no," Dora sighed. "The path to the Pond is blocked by vines and prickly leaves."

"How will we get through?" Boots asked.

"You can ssslither like me," hissed a snake, popping his head out of the bushes. "If you ssslither, you'll ssslide under those vines and prickly leaves."

Dora said, "Great idea! Let's slither like a snake. *Slither! Slither! Slither!*"

Swing! Swing! Swing!

Hop! Hop! Hop!

Ssslither! Ssslither! Ssslither!

After they slithered under the vines, Dora
invited the snake to go with them to the Animal Parade.
Everyone continued toward the Pond.
"We're going to the Animal Parade!" hissed the snake.

Finally, Dora, Boots, the frog, and the snake reached the Pond.

"Look! I see a boat!" Dora exclaimed. "We can use the boat to get across the Pond."

"But the boat is buried in the dirt. How will we get it out?" wondered Boots.

Suddenly a little mole popped out of the ground and said, "I can help. Just dig like me. *Dig! Dig! Dig!*"

Dora said, "Great idea! Let's dig like a mole. *Dig! Dig! Dig!*"

March!

MARch!

MArch!

After they dug the boat out of the dirt, everyone dragged the boat to the edge of the Pond. Then Dora invited the mole to go with them to the Animal Parade. "We're going to the Animal Parade!" squealed the mole.

Out in the middle of the Pond, Dora, Boots, the frog, the snake, and the mole soon found themselves surrounded by lily pads.

"Our boat is stuck!" cried Dora.

Just then a duck swam up to them and said, "Paddle like me to keep your boat moving."

Dora said, "Great idea! Let's paddle like a duck. *Paddle! Paddle! Paddle!*"

March!
March!
March!

After paddling to the other side of the Pond, Dora
invited the duck to go with them to the Animal Parade.
Everyone continued toward the Rocky Canyon.
"We're going to the Animal Parade!" quacked the Duck.

When they got to the Rocky Canyon, Boots shouted, "We're almost at the Animal Parade. But it's on the other side of the canyon."

"Hmm," thought Dora. "We'll need some help to get over the canyon."

Just then two large birds flew by and said, "We'll fly you over the canyon. But you'll need to flap like us to help us fly."

Dora said, "Great idea! Everybody flap like birds. *Flap! Flap! Flap!*"

After they flew over the Rocky Canyon, Dora invited the birds to go with them to the Animal Parade.

"Look at the crowd!" said Boots.

"Let's follow them to the Animal Parade," sang the birds.

Animal Parade!

March!
March!
March!

All of a sudden Dora, Boots, the frog, the snake, the mole, the duck, and the birds heard lots of clapping.

"Look!" Dora shouted, "We're not just going to watch the parade, we're *in* the Animal Parade!"

The townspeople cheered and cheered.
Everyone loved the Animal Parade!